X-MEN

ENTER THE X-MEN

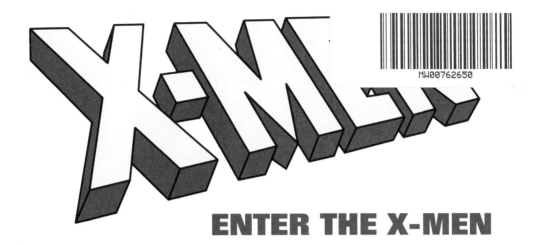

based on a teleplay by Mark Edward Edens
illustrated by Marie Severin
cover painting by Lourdes Sanchez

NOTE TO READER: Definitions for underlined words can be found in the glossary at the back of the book.

Random House  **New York**

Copyright © 1993 by Marvel Entertainment Group, Inc. All rights reserved under International and Pan-American Copyright Conventions.
Published in the United States by Random House, Inc., New York, and simultaneously in Canada by Random House of Canada Limited, Toronto.
Library of Congress Catalog Card Number: 93-86033 ISBN: 0-679-85707-9
Manufactured in the United States of America 10 9 8 7 6 5 4 3

While Jubilee's foster parents argued...
HOW COULD YOU HAVE REGISTERED HER WITH THE MUTANT CONTROL AGENCY?
LET'S JUST HOPE THE NEIGHBORS NEVER FIND OUT OUR BEAUTIFUL JUBILEE'S A MUTANT.

…Jubilee was upstairs listening.
Was it her fault that sometimes when she laid hands on a machine, <u>plasmoids</u> shot out of her fingers, destroying everything she touched?

At that very moment, a giant robot called a <u>Sentinel</u> was stalking Jubilee.

But later that evening, the robot came up empty-handed!

On the way out, Jubilee ran into a couple of shoppers. But not just any shoppers. They were the <u>X-Men</u> Storm and Rogue!

WHAT'S YOUR HURRY, SUGAH?

OUTTA MY WAY!

Suddenly, a towering Sentinel crashed through the mall's glass wall.

DO NOT BE ALARMED! I AM HERE TO SERVE AND PROTECT!

Storm flew at the robot, freeing Jubilee.

STORM, MISTRESS OF THE ELEMENTS, COMMANDS YOU TO RELEASE THE CHILD!

Then Rogue took over and sent the robot flying.

DID YOU SEE THAT?

ROGUE HAS A WAY WITH MEN.

Meanwhile, Gambit rushed to the scene.

STAND ASIDE. I MUST APPREHEND THE MUTANT.

APPREHEND THIS!

Jubilee ran, but the Sentinel gassed her. She choked and staggered.

Cyclops caught her!

OH, NO!

ENERGY BLAST, EH? HERE'S ONE FROM A PRO.

Waking up in a strange bed, Jubilee got up to find out where she was.

She caught sight of a strange man. This was the <u>mutant</u> known as Beast.

IT WOULD BE MOST DISCONCERTING IF THIS WERE TO EXPLODE . . .DISCONCERTING BUT PROVOCATIVE.

Moving on, she observed yet another mutant.

This one kept changing his form.

MY FELLOW AMERICANS: I AM AN IDIOT.

Then two other mutants discovered she was on the loose. They sounded an alarm.

THE GIRL! SHE'S TRYING TO RUN AWAY!

I KNEW WE COULDN'T HIDE THE EXISTENCE OF THE X-MEN FOREVER.

Jubilee ran into a room. Doors shut behind her. Suddenly, she was surrounded by flashing lights. Gambit was being attacked by a fierce clawed mutant.

INITIATE WOLVERINE-GAMBIT TRAINING SEQUENCE.

SWOOSH

Jubilee knocked Gambit's assailant to the floor.

ZAP

Just then the doors slid open. The other X-Men stood there, laughing at the sight of the mighty Wolverine knocked flat by a gutsy teen.

Storm took Jubilee up on the mansion roof and explained everything.

WE ARE MUTANTS, LIKE YOURSELF. PROFESSOR X IS OUR LEADER, AND HE HAS NAMED US THE X-MEN. THIS IS PROFESSOR XAVIER'S SCHOOL FOR GIFTED YOUNGSTERS, WHERE WE LEARN TO CONTROL OUR MUTANT POWERS FOR THE BENEFIT OF MANKIND.

Later, Professor Xavier called the X-Men together. He had discovered a photograph of Jubilee stored in the computer banks of the robot they had brought back from the mall.

THIS PHOTO COMES FROM THE MUTANT CONTROL AGENCY'S ID REGISTRATION FILES. THAT'S HOW THE SENTINELS FOUND HER.

Meanwhile, Jubilee had sneaked home to warn her parents. But she walked right into…a Sentinel ambush!

NOT AGAIN!

Henry Peter Gyrich, the head of the <u>Mutant Control Agency</u> himself, looked on coldly.

MUTANT APPREHENDED.

GOOD WORK!

Back at the mansion, Jean interrupted the meeting with the news that Jubilee had left. But there was no time to rescue one mutant when hundreds were in danger.

The X-Men flew that very night to the headquarters of the Mutant Control Agency, where they set Professor X's plan into action.

Storm whipped up a rainstorm.

Beast heaved Morph over the fence. Morph transformed himself into a guard.

Once inside the fence, Wolverine ripped open the door like a can of sardines.

SHREKKK!

Beast shut off the alarm system.

Then the team set to work trashing the files.

Their mission accomplished, they prepared to leave. But it wasn't going to be that easy.

CYCLOPS, WE'RE COMING OUT!

Sure enough, armed guards were swarming everywhere. Sentinels loomed before them. Wolverine ran boldly toward one.

Back at the mansion, Jean Grey stiffened and cried out.

Her senses had just sent her a message.

Breathlessly, the retreating team stood by their jet, the Blackbird, and took stock. When last seen, Beast was snared in an electric fence, outnumbered by guards. No one was sure what had become of Morph.

But Wolverine had other ideas. He was heading back for Beast and Morph.

As Wolverine started to run, Cyclops gave the signal to Rogue. Rogue touched Wolverine on the shoulder. Wolverine slumped. Her idea was to drain the energy out of him with her power…just enough to stop him but not enough to hurt him.

Wolverine fell to the ground, helpless.

GLOSSARY

mutant: A person born with strange abilities, far beyond those of ordinary humans. A mutant can look like an average human being or not, depending on the particular mutation. Many people are afraid of mutants and their powers.

Mutant Control Agency: A government organization set up to find mutants, keep track of them, and capture them if they harm anyone. It is run by Henry Peter Gyrich, who hates mutants and thinks they should all be imprisoned.

plasma: A mixture of energy and gas, like that found in the sun.

plasmoids: Bursts of plasma such as those produced by Jubilee and released through her fingertips.

Sentinel: Giant robot created by the Mutant Control Agency to hunt and catch mutants.

X-Men: A group of mutants brought together by Professor Charles Xavier. Their goal is to protect both humans and mutants from those mutants who would do them harm. They seek to promote peaceful coexistence between humans and mutants. They are sworn to protect a world that often fears and hates them. Led by Storm and Cyclops, the current membership includes Wolverine, Jubilee, Rogue, Gambit, and Jean Grey.